14 Days

NOV. 13 1990
MAY 18 1991
JUN 1 1991
JUN 8 1991
SEP 18 1991
JUN 30 1992
DEC 1 1993
JUL 25 1994
SEP 3 1994
JUN 16 1995
JUN 24 1995
JUN 28 1996
AUG 3 1996
FEB 19 1997
FEB 19 1997
JAN 25 2000
JUN 21 2000
NOV 20 2000
MAR 26 2001
DEC 13 2001
JUL 11 '06
JUL 14 '06
JUL 17 '08

WITHDRAWN

W9-AMO-793

The Mystery Of The Missing Scarf

WRITTEN BY MARY BLOUNT CHRISTIAN
ILLUSTRATED BY JOE BODDY

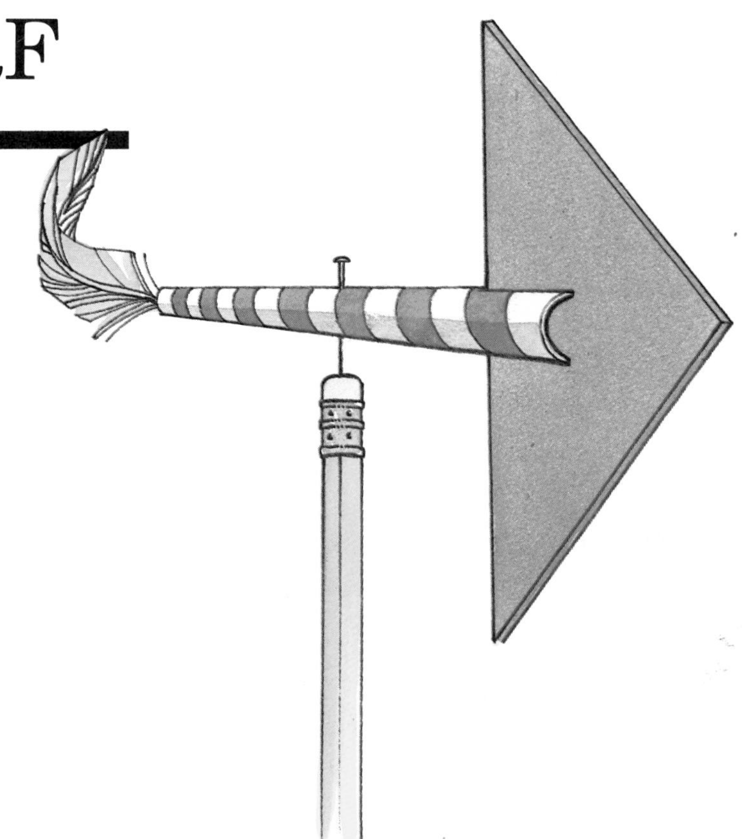

Milliken Publishing Company, St. Louis, Missouri

© 1989 by Milliken Publishing Company

All rights reserved. No part of this book may be used or reproduced in any manner whatsoever without written permission. Printed in the United States of America.

Cover Design by Henning Design, St. Louis, Missouri

Library of Congress Catalog Card Number: 88-60630
ISBN 0-88335-549-3 (pbk.)/ISBN 0-88335-596-5 (lib. bdg.)

"Look, Ann," Walter told his sister.
"Watch the new trick I taught Watson."

"I can't watch now," Ann said.
"My scarf is dirty, so I need to wash it.
Besides, you can't teach that silly dog anything."

j 40812

"But I did teach him a trick!
Watch!" Walter said.
Walter held a rag in the air.
Watson jumped up and snatched the rag.
He shook it and then ran off with it.

Ann laughed. “That’s not much of a trick.”

Walter frowned. “I will show
Pedro and David the trick later.
I bet they will like it.”

“We’ll see,” Ann said. “Wait for me.
I’ll go with you as soon as I wash my scarf.”

Ann ran warm water in the sink
and shook soap into the water.
She washed her scarf in the soapy water.

"Hurry up!" her brother Walter called.

"I'm coming as soon as I hang
my scarf out to dry," Ann said.

Ann squeezed the water from
her scarf and took it outside.
She did not have clothespins,
so she hung her scarf over the line
so that its edges touched.
"It is windy today, so my scarf
will dry quickly," she told Walter.

Ann and Walter walked to Pedro's house, with Watson close behind. David was already there.

"Watch our great new trick!" said Walter, holding up the rag. Watson snatched the rag and ran home with it. David laughed. "Well, that's pretty good."

"It is for Watson anyway,"
Pedro said, laughing too.
"Now I want to show you something,"
Pedro said, holding up a small box.
Walter looked into the box.
He saw a feather, a straw, a pencil,
a piece of cardboard, a straight pin,
and a pair of scissors.

"What are you doing with
those things?" he asked Pedro.

"I am making a weather vane," Pedro said.

"What a perfect day to try it out!" Ann said.

Pedro cut a long triangle from the cardboard.

"That looks like an arrowhead," David said.

"That will point to where the wind is coming from," Pedro told them.

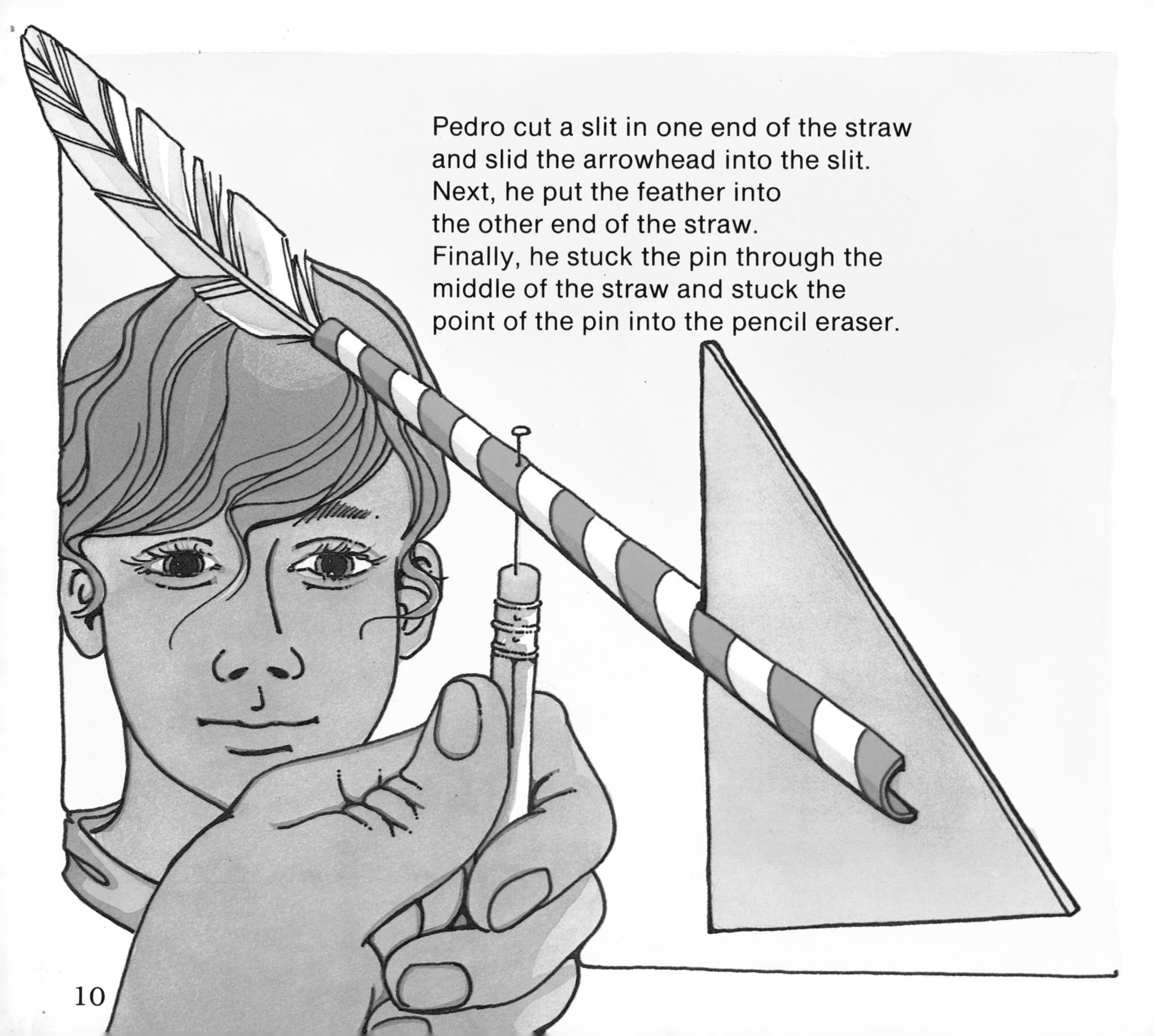

Pedro cut a slit in one end of the straw
and slid the arrowhead into the slit.
Next, he put the feather into
the other end of the straw.
Finally, he stuck the pin through the
middle of the straw and stuck the
point of the pin into the pencil eraser.

"But how does it work?" David asked.

"The wind blows against the feather," Pedro said. "When the feather stops moving, the arrow will point to where the wind is coming from."

Ann laughed. "But I already know where the wind is coming from! See? The trees are bending away from the wind."

"Yes," Pedro said, "the blowing trees do show the direction of the wind. But this weather vane will be more exact." Pedro tied the pencil to the top of a long straight stick. Then he stuck the other end of the stick into the ground. The feather swung around.

Ann said, "I must go home now.
I want to see if my scarf is dry."

Soon Ann was back. She was very angry.
"My scarf is gone!" she said.
"Watson took my scarf.
What a dumb trick you have taught him,"
she told Walter.

Ann ran home. Walter ran after her.
David and Pedro ran after Walter.
"Watson," Walter called.

Watson came to Walter.
He rolled on his back and wiggled.
"Do you have Ann's scarf?"
Walter asked Watson.
"Show me where it is.
Fetch Ann's scarf, Watson."

Watson sat up and barked, "Woof! Woof!"
He licked Walter's hand.

Walter looked under the bed.
He looked in the closet.
He looked everywhere Watson
might have taken Ann's scarf.
"I do not think Watson has
your scarf," Walter said.

"Then where is it?"
Ann asked.

Pedro asked, "Where was your scarf the last time you saw it, Ann?"

"Yes!" David said. "You must start where you last saw it. Show us, Ann."

Ann took the boys into the backyard.
Watson ran after them, barking, "Woof! Woof!"

Ann pointed. "It was right there, hanging
on the clothesline. And now it's gone!
I'm sure Watson took my scarf."

"Hmmm," Pedro said.
"This is a good mystery
and we are good detectives.
Let the Sherlock Street Detectives
look for your scarf."

"What a good idea!" Walter said. He pulled his notebook and his pencil from his pocket. "Tell us everything you know about your scarf."

"Well," Ann said, "it was a gift from
Aunt Nita for my birthday last year."

"We don't want to know that!" David said.
"We want to know things that will
help us solve the mystery.
What did the scarf look like?
What was it doing out here?
And what happened to the clothespins
that held it to the line?"

Ann shrugged. "It was white
with pink flowers on it.
It was on the line because I washed it.
And there were no clothespins."

Walter wrote in his notebook:

White with pink flowers.
Scarf washed.
No pins to hold it.

1. White with
pink flowers
2. Scarf washed
No pins to
hold it

"I think I see one problem already," Walter said. "Your scarf blew away because you did not pin it to the clothesline."

"No, the scarf was very heavy," Ann said. "It stayed on the line by itself."

"It was heavy because it was wet," David said. "The water made it heavy. But when it dried, it was not heavy. Then it blew away."

"Oh, no!" Ann said. "You're right! Now my scarf has blown away! How will I ever find it?"

"We will use my weather vane," Pedro said.
"We will see which way the wind is blowing.
Then we will look in that direction for
your scarf."

j 40812

Pedro ran home to get his weather vane.
When he came back, he stuck it in the
ground under the clothesline.
The arrow spun around.
It pointed toward the Brights' house.
"Remember," Pedro said, "the arrow
points to where the wind came from."
The children looked at the feather.
It pointed toward David's house.
The children ran to David's house
and looked and looked.

"Woof! Woof!" Watson said.
He was barking at a bush.

"Look!" Walter said.
"There is your scarf!
It's in the bush.
Watson found your scarf.
He didn't take your scarf."

Ann took her scarf from the bush.
"I am sorry I said you took
my scarf, Watson," Ann said.
"I will not be so fast to
blame you next time."
She patted Watson on the head.

"Woof! Woof!" he said.
He jumped up and snatched
the scarf from Ann's hand.
Then he ran off with it.

"Oh, no!" Ann said, laughing.
"I guess Watson really did learn
the trick you taught him, Walter."

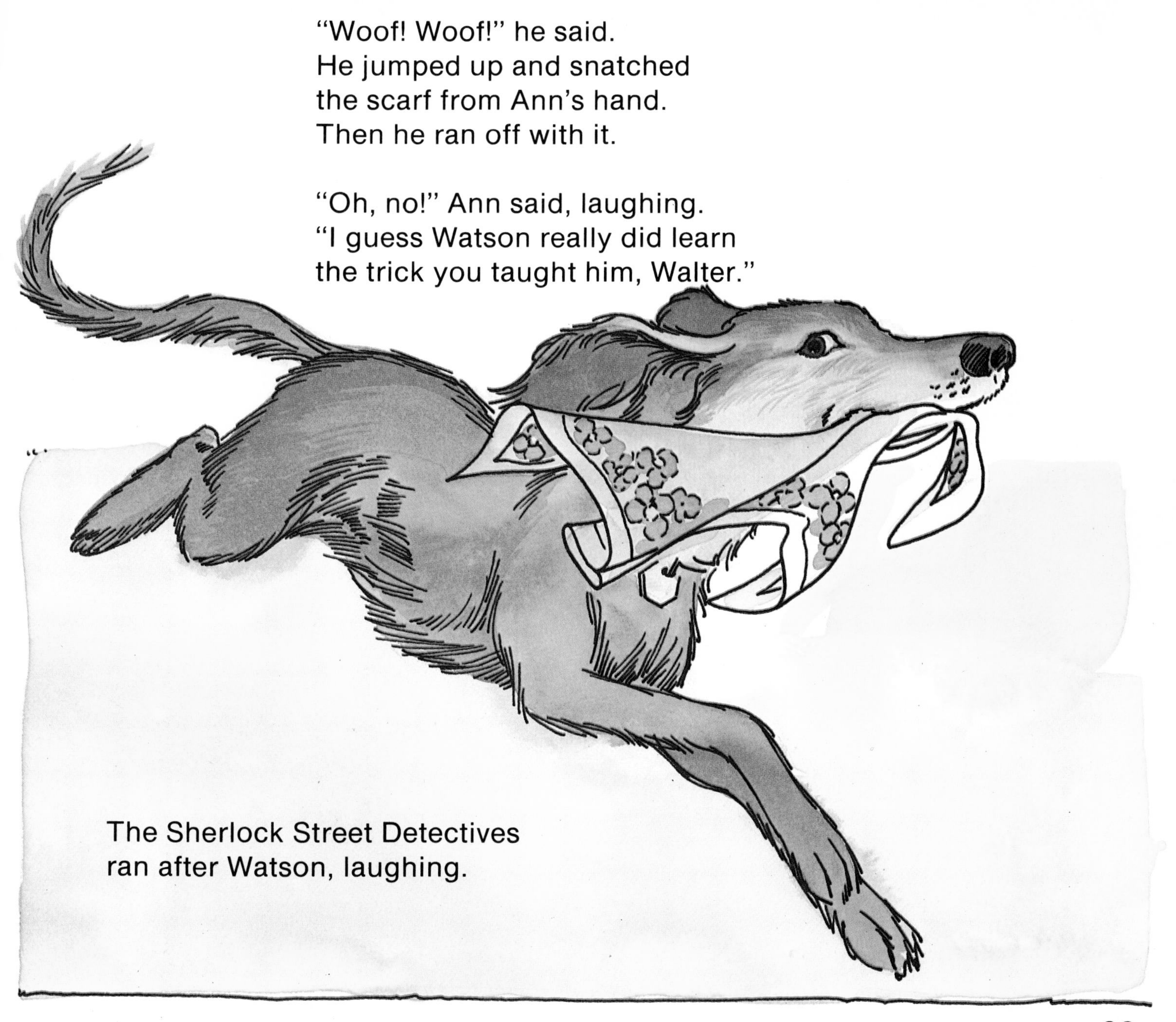

The Sherlock Street Detectives
ran after Watson, laughing.

Glossary

arrowhead – The pointed tip of an arrow.

direction – The path along which something moves.

weather vane – A pointer that turns in the wind. It shows which way the wind is blowing.

Vocabulary

against
air
already
angry
Ann
anything
anyway
around
arrow
arrowhead
Aunt Nita
backyard
barked
barking
behind
bending
besides
birthday
blame
blew
blowing
blown
blows
Brights
brother
bush
cardboard
children
close
closet
clothesline
clothespins
David
detectives
direction
dirty
does
dried
dry
dumb
edges
eraser
everything
everywhere
exact
feather
fetch
finally
flowers
found
frowned
gift
gone
great
ground
guess
hang
hanging
happened
head
heavy
house
hung
hurry
idea
itself
know
laughed
laughing
learn
licked
middle
might
more
moving
mystery
notebook
other
pair
patted
Pedro
pencil
perfect
piece
pocket
point(s)
pointed
pretty
problem
pulled
quickly
really
remember
rolled
scarf
scissors
Sherlock
shook
shrugged
silly
sink
snatched
soap
soapy
solve
something
sorry
spun
squeezed
stayed
stick
straight
straw
street
stuck
sure
swung
taught
things
those
through
tied
touched
toward
triangle
trick
vane
Walter
warm
watch
water
Watson
we'll
weather
wiggled
year